Anneena came round to play with Biff and
Chip. Wilf and Wilma came too, and so did
Nadim.

"I'm six next week," Kipper told them. "Do you
want to come to my birthday?"

"Six? You're catching up with me," said Wilma.

Mum took Kipper to the shops. When he had gone, Wilma had an idea.

"Let's form a band. Then we can play Happy Birthday to Kipper."

"But his birthday is next week," said Nadim.

"We'll need the time to practise," said Wilma.

Biff liked the idea of forming a band. The boys
were not so sure.

"We can't play instruments," said Wilf.

"You and Chip can play the kazoo," said Biff.
"Nadim can play the tambourine."

"And we can all sing," said Anneena.

At last they were ready to play. Wilma started
them off. "One … two … three," she said.

They began to play Happy Birthday.

It sounded quite good. It sounded even better
when they played it again.

Suddenly the magic key began to glow.

The magic took the children on another
adventure.

"Help!" called Anneena. "We still have our
instruments."

"I hope my guitar doesn't get broken," said
Wilma.

The magic took the children back in time. It
took them to the Middle Ages.

"Who are those people?" asked Nadim. "Why
are they doing tricks?"

"They must be entertainers," said Anneena.
"I think they are practising."

At first the entertainers didn't see the children. They went on practising.

The juggler kept dropping the balls. The girl on stilts held on to the tree.

"If they're entertainers, they're not very good," said Biff. "No wonder they're practising."

One of the entertainers saw the children. He ran across to them.

"My name is John," he said. "You must be musicians."

"We're not proper musicians," said Wilma.

"I have a job for you," said the man.

"But ... but ...," said Biff.

The man looked at Wilma's guitar.

"What a strange instrument," he said.

The girl looked at Biff's recorder.

"What a strange pipe," she said.

"You look a bit young to be musicians," said John. "You'd better play us a tune."

Suddenly a man on a horse rode up. He looked very cross.

"Are you the entertainers?" he shouted. "You should be at the castle by now."

"The musicians were late," said John. "But we are ready now."

"Then hurry!" said the man. "The Duke hates to be kept waiting."

He peered at the children.

"Are these the musicians?" he asked. "They look very young."

"They are the finest in the land," said John.

"But ... but ...," stammered Wilma.

The man made everyone go to the castle. The children ran behind.

"How can we entertain the Duke?" Biff said. "We're not proper musicians."

"Don't worry," said John. "I bet you can play something. You *all* have instruments."

"We can only play one song," said Nadim. "It's called Happy Birthday. You only play it on someone's birthday."

"I don't know it," said John, "but it sounds perfect. It *is* the Duke's birthday. That's why we're going to entertain him."

The Duke was waiting with his wife and
daughter. They looked at the entertainers.

The entertainers gave a low bow.

The Duke's daughter looked surprised.

"We'd better bow as well," whispered Wilf.
"It's not every day we meet a duke."

The Duke peered at the children.

"The musicians are very young," he said.

"They are the finest in the land," said John.

"They had better be good," said the Duke. "I am very fond of music."

"They have made up a song for you," said John.

The entertainers went to practise. They were still not very good.

"They're terrible," said Nadim. "I don't think they're proper entertainers. Something funny is going on."

"Look out, here comes the Duke's daughter," said Wilf.

The Duke's daughter ran up to one of the
entertainers. She gave him a hug.

"Oh, Hugh! I'm so glad you're here," she said.

"I said I would find a way," said Hugh.

"You see!" said Nadim. "I said something
funny was going on."

The Duke's daughter was called Edith. She and Hugh were in love.

"We are not really entertainers," said John. "We are here to help Edith."

"My father won't let me marry yet," said Edith, "so we want to run away."

"Why pretend you are entertainers," said Chip, "when you are so terrible at it?"

"This was the only way we could get into the castle," said Hugh.

"Please help us," said John.

"Oh, all right," said Anneena.

Hugh gave Edith a bottle of sleeping mixture.

"Pour this mixture into the wine," he said. "Do it before the feast begins tonight."

"It will send everyone to sleep," said John. "Then we can get away safely."

Edith took the bottle. "Leave it to me," she said.

The entertainers made the children dress up.
"I feel silly, dressed like this," moaned Chip.
"You need to look the part," said John.
"Won't everyone be asleep?" asked Anneena.
"We hope so," said John.

It was time for the Duke's feast. Many people were there.

Servants took in great dishes of food. There was plenty of wine for everyone to drink.

Edith was worried. She had put the sleeping mixture into the wine, but no one had fallen asleep.

Now it was time for the entertainment.

"This is not part of my plan," hissed John.
"Why has no one fallen asleep?"

"The mixture isn't working," said Chip.

"What shall we do now?" asked Hugh.

"We'll just have to entertain them," said John.

The entertainers were terrible. Everyone began to shout and throw food at them. The Duke was angry.

"Entertainers?" he shouted. "You are terrible. I'll put you in the dungeons."

"Wait!" begged John. "Please hear the musicians. They are the finest in the land."

The children got ready to play. Wilma started
them off.

"One ... two ... three," she said.

They began to play Happy Birthday.

It sounded quite good. It sounded even better
when they played it again.

The people clapped and cheered.

"Excellent," said the Duke. "Play it again."
Wilma had an idea. She whispered to Hugh.
"Creep out now and take Edith."
Then she clapped her hands.
"This time I am going to teach you the words,"
she said. "You can all join in."

Wilma taught everyone the words to Happy
Birthday.

Edith slipped away. No one saw her go.
Everyone was singing loudly.

"You *are* the finest in the land," said the Duke.
"What other tunes can you play?"

Hugh and Edith escaped from the castle. There were some horses waiting for them.

"Tomorrow we will get married," said Hugh. "Do you think your father will give you his blessing?"

"Of course he will," said Edith, "when he sees how happy we are."

"This note is from Edith," said the Duke. "She has run away to get married. I suppose we should chase after her."

Suddenly the Duke gave a yawn.

"I feel very sleepy," he said. "Maybe I'll chase after her when I've had a snooze."

"Everyone is asleep," said Wilma. "So the sleeping mixture worked in the end."

The magic key began to glow.

"What a strange end to the adventure," said Chip. "There's no one left awake to say goodbye to."

The magic took them home.

"We don't need to practise Happy Birthday again," said Nadim. "We're pretty good at it."

Then Kipper came in.

"What have you all been doing?" he asked.

"Just messing about," said Biff.

It was Kipper's sixth birthday. The band played
Happy Birthday.

"That was brilliant," said Kipper. "I didn't
know you were such good musicians."

"Of course we are," said Wilma. "We're the
finest in the land."